*For a teacher called Stuart, who started the day by getting Yellow Class
to sing the old campfire "Hippo Song"... and gave me the idea for this story – ST*

For all the imaginary animals we dreamed of, that liked having their backs scratched ... – LC

JANETTA OTTER-BARRY BOOKS

Text copyright © Sean Taylor 2014
Illustrations copyright © Laurent Cardon 2014
The rights of Sean Taylor and Laurent Cardon to be identified respectively as the author and
illustrator of this work have been asserted by them in accordance with the Copyright,
Designs and Patents Act, 1988 (United Kingdom).

First published in Great Britain and in the USA in 2014 by
Frances Lincoln Children's Books, 74-77 White Lion Street, London N1 9PF
www.franceslincoln.com

A catalogue record for this book is available from the British Library.

ISBN 978-1-84780-455-6

Illustrated with mixed ink techniques and digital art

Printed in China

1 3 5 7 9 8 6 4 2

That's What Makes a Hippopotamus Smile!

Written by
Sean Taylor

Illustrated by
Laurent Cardon

F

FRANCES LINCOLN
CHILDREN'S BOOKS

When a hippopotamus comes round to your house, don't be worried, or *scared* by his **size**.
Just hug him and open the door very w i d e .

Because . . .

. . . that's what makes
a hippopotamus come inside!

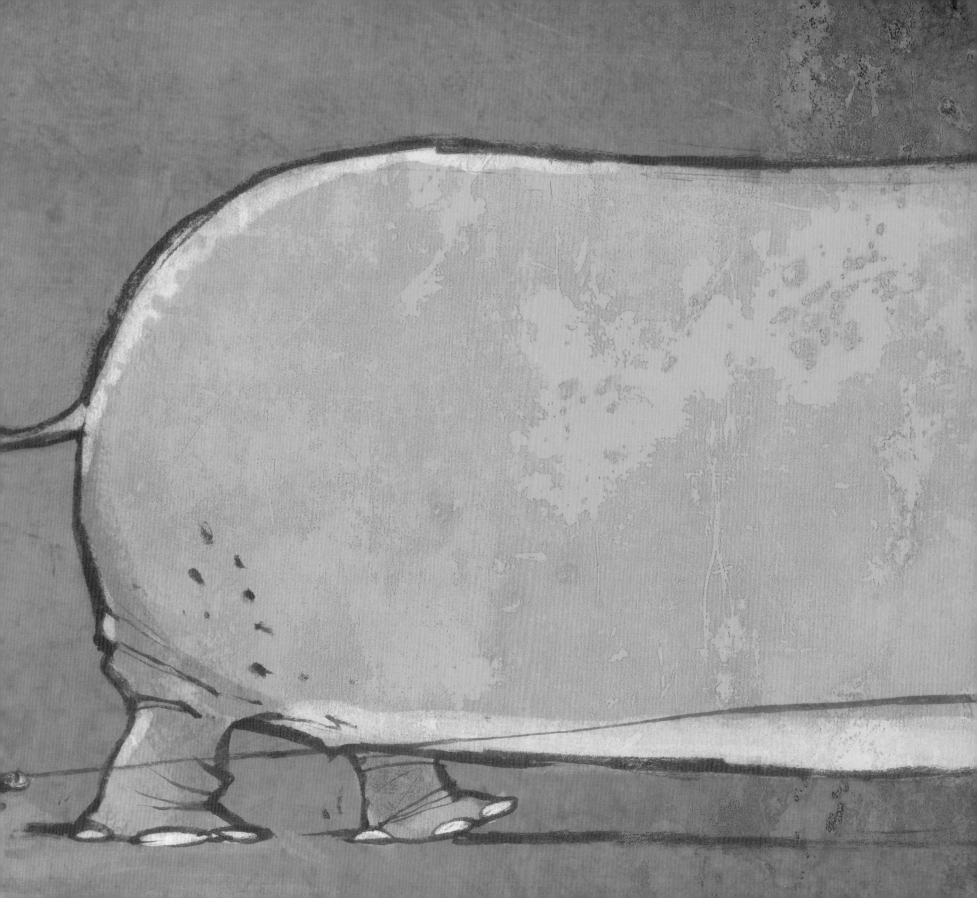

And when a hippopotamus wants to play a game, don't make it quiet, clean or dry.
Choose something **splishy, sploshy** and **splashy**.

Because . . .

. . . that's what makes
a hippopotamus happy!

When you and the hippo need cleaning up,
remember that hippos love a good wash.
So share silly toys in a **big warm** bath.

Because . . .

... that's what makes
a hippopotamus laugh!

And after that, you'll both be hungry.
But don't eat popcorn, cookies or chips.
Have a great BIG crunchy salad-treat.

Because . . .

. . . that's what a hippopotamus
loves to eat!

And when the hippo has to go home,
try not to be sad . . . even if you are.
Do a little dance.

Say goodbye in style.
Because . . .

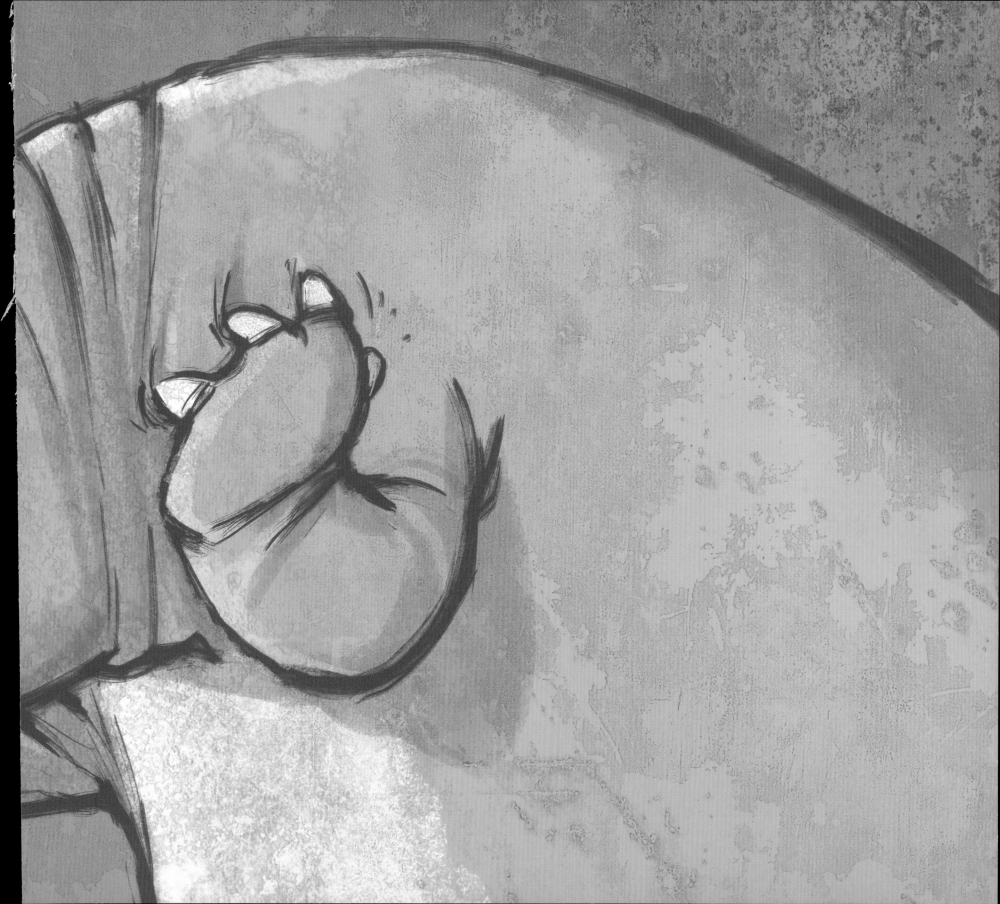

. . . that's what makes
a hippopotamus smile!

Then when the hippo thinks about you,
and of all the fun the two of you had,
he'll know that you're his
BEST NEW FRIEND.

And . . .

...**that's** what makes
a hippopotamus
come **round again!**

(Though maybe not just on his own . . .)